CW00863019

# A True Love Story

## A Self-Esteem Builder
### STORY AND WORKBOOK

by **Janice Quashie**
**Illustrations by Richard Brown**

**TRAFFORD**
PUBLISHING

Note for Librarians: A cataloguing record for this book is available from Library and Archives
Canada at www.collectionscanada.ca/amicus/index-e.html
ISBN 1-4120-9589-1

*Printed in Victoria, BC, Canada. Printed on paper with minimum 30% recycled fibre.*
*Trafford's print shop runs on "green energy" from solar, wind and other environmentally-friendly*
*power sources.*

*Offices in Canada, USA, Ireland and UK*

**Book sales for North America and international:**
Trafford Publishing, 6E–2333 Government St.,
Victoria, BC V8T 4P4 CANADA
phone 250 383 6864 (toll-free 1 888 232 4444)
fax 250 383 6804; email to orders@trafford.com
**Book sales in Europe:**
Trafford Publishing (UK) Limited, 9 Park End Street, 2nd Floor
Oxford, UK OX1 1HH UNITED KINGDOM
phone +44 (0)1865 722 113 (local rate 0845 230 9601)
facsimile +44 (0)1865 722 868; info.uk@trafford.com
**Order online at:**
trafford.com/06-1345

10 9 8 7 6 5 4 3 2

# A True Love Story

## Contents

A Special Dedication. . . . . . . . . . . . . . . . . . . . . 5

Acknowledgements. . . . . . . . . . . . . . . . . . . . 6

Introduction . . . . . . . . . . . . . . . . . . . . . . . . . 7

## Section 1

A True Love Story

By Janice Quashie . . . . . . . . . . . . . . . . . . . . . . .11

## Section 2

A True Love Story Work book . . . . . . . . . . . . . . .27

## Section 3

My True Love Story. . . . . . . . . . . . . . . . . . . . . .77

## Section 4

Your True Love Story . . . . . . . . . . . . . . . . . . . . .83

Contact Details. . . . . . . . . . . . . . . . . . . . . . . . .97

# A Special Dedication

To God I give the highest honour for blessing me with the creative ability to write this book. May this book do what you intended it to, may it touch and change the lives of all who read it for the better.

To my husband, Ian, thank you for your love and support, and for the terrific photograph, you are truly awesome, and I love you.

Lauren you were a great listener, advisor, and encourager, mother salutes you. To my mother, (Queen Esther), for always encouraging me to do my best and for leading the way. To my brothers Robert and Jeremy, for allowing me to just be me. To my brother Lenford for constantly being such a reliable helper, listener, encourager and common sense friend, I love you much. To the Quashie family and the Slough/High Wycombe massive, thank you for prayers, advice and the means to let off steam.

To Richard Brown, whose illustrations and vocal talents brought this book and Quentin to life. To Debbie, your professional manner kept us on track, I love you both dearly.

A special mention to Ivell, Sherilyn, Harriett, Carol, Tracy, The New Testament Church of God, Mile End and the Complete Women team, for your prayer support, love, listening ears, sound boarding and encouragement. You were always there when I needed you.

To Jacqueline Peart, for continually affirming, encouraging, praying and inspiring me, I love and respect you as a woman after God's own heart. Thank you, Mum, Dad, Marcia and Yvonne for adopting me into the Peart family, it means a lot. To Phil, Cem, Diane and Michael for our online chats, they blessed me more than you will ever know. To the ladies of the Black Unity Forum, for allowing me to flow and grow with you. Keep hold of your dreams, keep working on making them a reality and do not forget to make time for yourselves.

To all those too numerous to name, God bless you.

# Acknowledgements

This book exists thanks to the kind financial contributions of the following:

Ivell Haastrup, Harriett Archer, Joanne Coolie, Tracy Weekes, Sherilyn Phillips, Phil Wright, Davina Edwards, Carol Hall, Lisa Williams, Andrea Mc Arthur, Janet Shockness, Debbie and Richard Brown, Elvin Langdon, Marva Waldron, Kevin Hanley, Judy Tomlin.

A special mention to James Cook , and Trafford Publishing in the UK and Canada. The whole team has made this a very enjoyable and achievable project. I have felt love , and seen devotion and care up and beyond the expected. I look forward to working with you all again real soon. James thank you for the phone calls, sound advice, encouragement, and the humour it really helped. To the graphic department, thank you for your added hard work. It all looks amazing.

Many of you gave sacrificially and I bless you this and for the continued support. I pray that God will reward you far above that which I could conceive. May you reap a harvest that is plentiful, may good health, peace and love be your companions on the road of life. Thank you for your gifts of love and for putting your faith into action.

# Introduction

You hold in your hands, my ultimate true love story. I was challenged by my good friend, (and now illustrator) Richard Brown, to write something that was not health related. Angered by the challenge, I set to work. The first draft was far from exciting, but after several rewrites, I completed the challenge.

Once finished, Richard read the story and asked to do the illustrations. I had no idea about what to expect and left Richard to express his creativity. I will never forget the moment I saw the drawings, I was blown away. A True Love Story came to life. I stopped dreaming and dared to believe that this day would come, and here it is.

The journey has been long and a complete eye opener. I must really thank and bless all those who gave me finance and prayed to make this dream a reality. Everything has a price, but this was worth every penny, sleepless night, rewrite and doubt.

It is amazing to believe in yourself; it is totally awesome when friends love and support you; but truly amazing to know that despite my mistakes and my faults God loves me unconditionally. That His love caused Him to freely give His son, Jesus, to die in my place, so that I would have life, now; that is the ultimate True Love Story.

Laughter brings you healing,

And fills the heart with cheer.

So let this story make you smile,

As love and romance, fill the air.

# A True Love Story

## Section 1

More than anything else in life Quentin wanted to be loved. He longed for the day when his extra crispy dry lips, would meet with the luscious ones of his dream girl. He stood tall and proud, a full figure of a five-foot man, red hair, green eyes, with a cuddly 14 stone chiselled physique. He wore his clothes with a style unique to him; so unique it could not be classified.

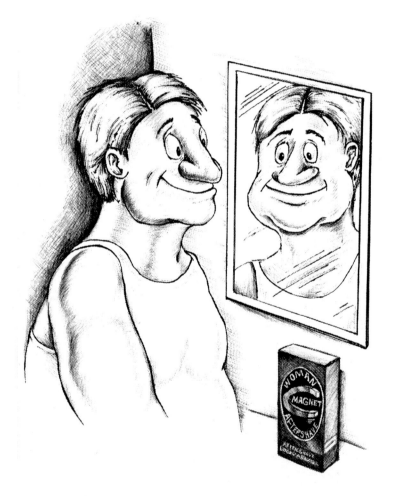

"Today," he told his reflection in the mirror,
"is the start of something new."

He pulled on his red trousers, yellow, blue and green
Hawaiian shirt, and brown leather shoes.

Splashing on a good dose of Woman Magnet aftershave, he
headed off into the sunshine to meet his fate.

Whistling, "She'll be coming round the mountain," he made good time to the tube station. He greeted several females with his special gummy smile and eye gesture, the one he was convinced, turned women's hearts and knees to jelly. As they beat a hasty retreat he told himself,
"Their loss, they are running away from a good thing."

No one could say that Quentin's self esteem was not high, but it was rather misplaced.

No one wanted to hurt his feelings, so Quentin was going through life, wearing very large rose tinted glasses.

As Quentin arrived at his job at the library, he was told by his colleagues that there was a lunchtime training session, and that all staff members were to be in attendance.

"Oh joy!" exclaimed Quentin,
"Will there be biscuits and sandwiches?"

As long as there was food at a meeting, the theme was irrelevant for Quentin.

He had a ritual of dissecting a custard cream biscuit with his teeth that had to be seen, to be believed.

Quentin spent the morning impatiently stamping and returning books, watching the clocks, repeatedly checking to see if they were working.
Lunchtime seemed to be taking a long time to arrive.

As the last fine was paid and the door locked, Quentin rushed on to the staff room, to claim his usual chair, at the back of the room, nearest the refreshment table.

As he came along the corridor he heard several voices, coming from the training room.

He had not been informed, that it was not a local branch meeting, but an annual general assembly, so he hurried along the corridor eagerly, without fear or anxiety.

As he opened the door, he was surprised to see a sea of unfamiliar faces, but he avoided eye contact and headed for his sanctuary corner.

As he manoeuvred through the crowds of talking people, Quentin was stopped dead in his tracks.

Sitting in his chair was a woman.

There she sat on his sacred spot, with her pad and pen poised and ready; looking calm, confident and comfortable.

Quentin's world was thrown into turmoil. His brain began to work over time hatching a plan to usurp the trespasser.

Feeling faint from the mental activity and nauseous from being separated from his chair, Quentin decided to go find his faithful friends, tea and biscuits.

Once fortified he decided to try again, in his quest to remove the smiling stranger.

As he glared at her, across the room, she moved her face in his direction, and their eyes met.

Quentin felt a strange sensation in his chest and he seemed to be loosing control of his body.

His mouth was forming a smile, his cheeks were feeling hot, and who told his feet to move anywhere?

Before he knew how, he was standing next to the woman,
and at that point he regained his bodily control.

He could hear the Woman saying,

"Hello my name's Clarissa."

But his speech had turned into some kind of unrecognisable babbling.

After much stammering and sweating Quentin finally took a breath and blurted out his name. "Qquuueeennttiinn."

Clarissa offered Quentin the seat next to hers. He reluctantly sat down and spent the whole meeting fidgeting. Every now and then the uncontrollable urges returned, and he found himself, sneaking a peak at Clarissa.

He traced the outline of her hair, and face in his mind. He sniffed the warmness of her perfume, and wondered if she liked custard creams.

Occasionally Clarissa would turn and see Quentin staring at her and the two would look away shyly.

During the icebreaker, Quentin and Clarissa found they had several things in common and laughed and giggled through the whole session.

The evaluation form filling drew near, signifying the end of the session. The strange sensation returned to Quentin's chest and he wondered if he dared ask for Clarissa's contact details.

As he was pondering Clarissa said:
"Oh well, it was good to meet you Quentin. Thank you for making this a memorable customer care session. Maybe we will meet up at the next annual general meeting."

Before Quentin could summon up enough spittle to lubricate his tongue, she floated past him and was gone.

He breathed a deep sigh, and looked slightly sad and reflective.

Then shaking himself he took a clean napkin, and cleaned off his beloved chair, caressing the arms, and legs with such tenderness.

"There, there now," he said, "if I have told you once, I have told you twice, there is only one love in my life and no Woman will ever come between us. I will make it up to you, I will bring in that upholstery cleaner, I know the one you like."

Giving her a parting squeeze he headed home, to reflect on how he would use his newfound customer care skills.

What? Did you expect Clarissa and Quentin to fall in love?

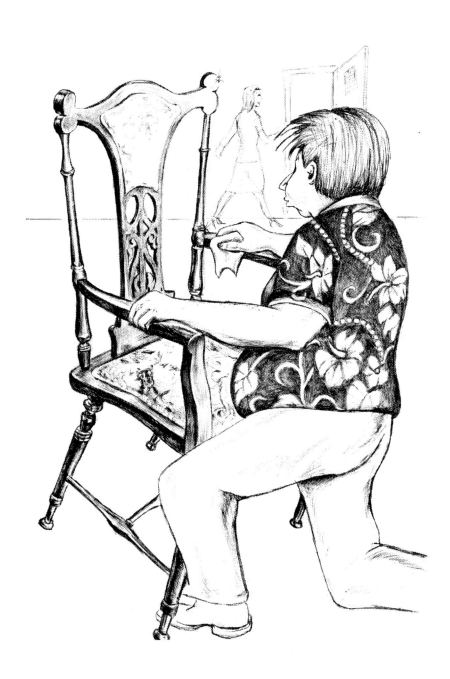

# A True Love Story

## WORKBOOK

## Section 2

# Introduction

This workbook is a self-help guide for all those who have challenges with their self-esteem, or need to boost their self worth and confidence.

This short study will take you through some key areas of self-development, that will:

- Encourage you to make the time to work on areas of underdeveloped potential.
- Enable you, to think positively about you, as a whole person.
- Empower you to become a more confident, assertive, happy individual.

Using A True Love Story, as a fun, yet informative training resource, your aims and objectives (on completion) will be to:

- Take a fresh look at who you are and what you stand for. (Personal development).
- Develop and maintain higher levels of self-esteem/ confidence.
- Develop better relationships, focusing on how you relate to others.
- Discover purpose/goals for your life; activating and fulfilling them.

# Your Personal Challenge

Many of you may have laughed at the unusual characteristics of Quentin, portrayed in "A True Love Story." If I asked you for your first impression of him, you have might have said that he was awkward, strange, on another planet and possibly weird. I **challenge** you to take to take a closer look. I believe you will discover that Quentin, has characteristics that many people go through life, trying to obtain.

Quentin is a confident, self-assured, well balanced, honest, focused, assertive, "in touch with his feelings," kind of guy.

Don't believe me? Before you laugh again, be prepared to look at things from a different angle.

You may find it helpful to have some of the following resources:

- notebook/journal/paper /folder /ring binder/computer or lap top file.
- pen/pencil/coloured pens/felt tips.

Remember this is your personal workbook. Keep your data safe and confidential. Try to spend quality time on each section. Reflect on what you have read. Come back to difficult areas. Take the time to be honest/open with yourself. If you struggle with any particular areas, ask yourself why. Invest time in finding out why you deny, get angry or dismiss things. Could there be some truth there? If yes, consider seeking help in coming to terms with things. If not, then move on. The more you put in, the more you will get out. There are no real right or wrong answers. Have fun while you learn a little more about you.

## Who You Are and What You Stand For (Personal Development)

**Personal** - one's own, individual, private.

**Development** - gradual unfolding, fuller, working out. Growth, expansion, progress, advance, increase, mature, improvement. Training, education, advancement, promotion, enhancement, event.

The Concise Oxford English Dictionary

Many people go through life having their first 18 years planned for them and then do their own thing for the next 22, often without too much planning. Then they reach 40 and begin to feel that life is drifting, they have no goals, and their dreams have not been realised. Mid life crisis they call it. For something or someone to develop it has to have a foundation. The plan then is to build on this core foundation, developing it, redesigning and adjusting it according to the changes that life and circumstances throw at you.

## Quentin the Man

### What do we learn about the character of Quentin?

You may find it helpful to re-read the story and think about:

1. Who Quentin is.
2. What does he think or believe?
3. What type of person does he want to be?

List his likes/dislikes, habits, positive, negative traits.
(Write notes below, or in your notebook). You can use these
notes to work on your personal development portfolio at a
later stage. If not just keep reading.

---

### Personal Development Portfolio Notes

...........................................................................................................

...........................................................................................................

...........................................................................................................

...........................................................................................................

...........................................................................................................

...........................................................................................................

...........................................................................................................

...........................................................................................................

...........................................................................................................

...........................................................................................................

...........................................................................................................

...........................................................................................................

...........................................................................................................

...........................................................................................................

...........................................................................................................

...........................................................................................................

...........................................................................................................

## Characteristics of Quentin: The Author's Findings

> **What do we learn about the character of Quentin?**

### Quentin has Personal Pride

He may not be the fashion world's idea of a supermodel, but Quentin works with what he has, he has **personal pride.** He expresses this in the way he walks, he holds his head up and faces the world. He walks with a sense of determination, he strides quickly making good progress. He has purpose in his step, places to go, people to see. He may be short in stature, but people are aware of his presence.

Many people think it is vain to be proud, but there is a fine line between being obsessed with yourself and valuing who you are. We are talking about being the best you, you can be inside and out. The alternative is the crazy trends to spend thousands of pounds, injecting fillers, having peels, or cosmetic surgery. Just like housework, once you begin work on the body, you will often begin to see other areas that need attention and maintenance is always necessary. Consider the effects these changes will have on your body with age and your wallet with time.

## Who am I and what do I stand for?

It is time to take a look at who you are.
Stand in front of a full length mirror...

Learn to appreciate your physical shape, it may not be perfect, but no one is. Make mental notes about you. Describe yourself positively. If you find this hard, ask yourself why.

(Most of us have fat bits, thin bits, cellulite, stretch marks, wrinkles and lack of muscle, but we want to concentrate on a more constructive image of ourselves; so leave these out for now).

Write your findings in the Personal Appreciation Questionnaire on the following page.

A tip from my friend Cheryl: she says before you leave your home in the morning, check your appearance, (front and back), in good light to see how you look. Remember white can be very see through, so wear something underneath if you do not want the world to see everything you have. Be careful in areas where there are strip lights as they will expose everything.

# Personal Appreciation Questionnaire

When I look at myself I see?

....................................................................................................

....................................................................................................

....................................................................................................

....................................................................................................

....................................................................................................

....................................................................................................

....................................................................................................

My best features are?

....................................................................................................

....................................................................................................

....................................................................................................

....................................................................................................

....................................................................................................

....................................................................................................

....................................................................................................

....................................................................................................

....................................................................................................

....................................................................................................

My body shape is?

.....................................................................................................

.....................................................................................................

.....................................................................................................

.....................................................................................................

.....................................................................................................

.....................................................................................................

.....................................................................................................

## Summary

1. It is important to know who you are, what you like, dislike and what you value.

2. Learning to appreciate your body image and working on the areas that cause you concern, will help you maintain a sense of well-being.

3. Take personal pride in yourself and the things that you do. Be the best that you can be.

## Develop and Maintain High Levels of Self-Esteem/Confidence

### Quentin has Self-Awareness

The Concise Oxford Dictionary defines self awareness as:

**Self** - person's or thing's own individuality or essence.

**Awareness** - Conscious, not ignorant, having knowledge, well informed.

**Self-awareness** - having knowledge about what makes you, you. Your physical, mental and psychological DNA.

Quentin is aware of who he is; he is confident about who he is. He neither looks for approval, nor craves it. There are levels of awareness, and you need to remember that your opinions, and outlook will change with age, and life experiences. Try to celebrate who you are through all these stages; if you don't, no-one else will and there is no way to turn back the clock and repeat stages.

### Outer Awareness

He is not afraid to dress in a way that makes him comfortable. His style may not be haute couture, but he is not a slave to fashion. He is not being dictated to by fashion gurus, who at times I believe, go out of the way to make the rich and famous look far from flattering.

Do you find yourself following catwalk fashion? Do you simply have to have the latest bag, or shoes? Image is important, but not at the expense of bearing all, crippling feet, or mortgaging the house to finance it. Think about it.

Quentin is not afraid of colour; he raises his spirits by wearing bold bright statements in clothing. I would suggest not wearing them all at the same time and consider skin tones, accessories and hair colouring when choosing an outfit.

Here are some interesting findings about colours and what they represent. Not scientific, but worth a read. The list is not exhaustive.

**Red,** a colour associated with boldness, passion, health, blood, danger, anger, confidence, assertiveness, energy. Red can cheer your mood, a warming colour. A great choice for coats, blankets and socks. In the world of health, eating foods that are red in colour are thought to have healing properties, especially when trying to fight infection. Men have been advised to eat red foods to prevent ailments like testicular/prostate cancer. Enjoy tomatoes, peppers, watermelon, cherries, strawberries, raspberries and cranberries - to combat symptoms of cystitis.

**Yellow,** the colour of optimism, intellect, stimulation, confidence, communication, inspiration, celebration. Yellow foods such as peppers, pineapples, lemons, grapefruit and mangoes, are thought to remove impurities from the blood.

**Gold** represents wealth, royalty, quality and wisdom.

**Pink** is the colour of love, romance, relaxation, feminity and passiveness.

**Green** signifies money, prosperity, wealth, employment. Fertility, growth, healing, relaxation. Nature, newness. Calmness.

**Orange** a combination of red and yellow. Energy, joy, creativity, success, stimulation, encouragement, youthfulness, warmth. Vibrancy.

**Purple** - healing, religion, regal, luxury. Sophistication, creativity, spirituality, positive affects on the mental condition increases self-belief and spiritual strength.

**Blue** - healing, peace, patience, happiness, calmness, royalty.

**Brown** - masculinity, stability, earth.

**White** - purity, innocence.

**Silver** - spiritual, wisdom, healing.

**Black** - protection, secretive.

## What image am I presenting?

What colours flatter you?

If your wardrobe contains a large number of dark colours and is strictly formal for the work environment, then why not brighten your outlook, with a splash of colour?

For men, a tie, shirt, or socks; for ladies a scarf, blouse, or jewellery. Try wearing colours on the weekend. Experiment with colour; take pieces of material and put them under your chin. Observe what each one does to your skin tone, whilst looking in a mirror. Avoid colours that make you look washed out, drained or tired looking; opt for colours that light up your features, enhance your eye/hair/ skin colouring and flatter you. Wear colour with pride.

Avoid wearing stripes, spots and checks altogether in the same outfit. Consider the effect on the eyes, of geometric patterns, dots and lines, even if they are black and white.

If you can afford it, enlist the help of a colour therapist or an image consultant.

Consider these simple rules:

- Be aware of your body shape.
- Wear appropriate undergarments to improve the way clothes look and fit you.
- For men, wear the right size and type of underwear; you now have the choice of boxers, Y-fronts, Tanga pants and for the very brave, thongs.
- Visible panty lines look just as bad on men, as they do on women.

Avoid the myth that one size fits all. When trying on clothes, look at yourself in a mirror from all angles. Be honest if you can't breathe or walk it's tooooo tight. If your body shape needs toning, don't wear clothes that highlight your problem areas, learn to disguise them until they become the shape you want. Consider wearing longer length jackets, skirts and dresses. Always try on garments before you buy them. Make sure that you buy the correct size, appropriate colours, and materials, as this will affect your over all look. Avoid trying to recapture your youth by wearing young fashions, unless you can really pull it off. Everyone has a fun outfit, but I would never recommend using it for everyday wear.

## Women's section (well worth a read Men!!!)

Before we leave outer awareness, let us look at some of
the different types of body shape that exist. It can be
very confusing when you start to look at all the various
classifications of body type and shape. I will stick to the
most basic information. This will help you to review the
types of clothes you should wear and that suit your body
type. Age, ill health, weight gain and loss will change your
physical shape so review this periodically.

Remember that most people are a combination of two or
more body types and this is quite normal. There are always
exceptions to every rule, if in doubt seek professional advice.

**Apple shaped** - Carry weight around the
chest, tummy/stomach. Avoid hipsters and figure hugging
garments. Opt for side zipped trousers/skirts; low-waisted,
single breasted jackets.

**Pear shaped** - Carry weight on upper
thighs/hips and around the bottom. It is trendy these days
to emphasise a well shaped bottom. Wearing boot cut/ wide
cut trousers can also be very flattering. Choose well fitted
clothing tailored to enhance the appearance.

**Hour glass** - Individuals with curves at the top and bottom, should wear well fitted (not tight), clothing. Tailored clothing will enhance your best physical assets.

**Willow/tall and slim** - Usually well/equally proportioned top and bottom. Athletic. Can wear most fashions. Individuals should avoid excessively baggy clothing. Low cut tops should be avoided unless you are wearing suitable under garments, or you have a bra cup size above B or C.

May I just say to all those who are aspiring to gain the perfect body, through endless diet, slimming potions, purging, medication, surgical intervention; please seek professional /medical help/support network. Maintain your weight with sensible eating habits, exercise and sessions of being good to yourself. Life is too short to try to pursue an impossible dream. There is no such thing as the perfect body. Love the one your in.

Ladies, just a quick note about shoes. Whilst there are some beautiful items of foot wear on the market, may I simply say, that if you buy high heels, please learn how to walk properly in them. There is nothing worse than a well dressed woman tottering, as if she is on stilts or looking like a cowboy missing his horse. Constantly wearing high heels could put pressure on your back, posture, pelvis and pressure on feet and ankles. Alternate your shoes, through the week, wearing a variety of heel heights. If you want to wear high heels but cannot walk in them gracefully, investigate wearing shoes with wedges or broader heels. Invest in gel soles, pedicure and general foot hygiene. Look after your feet and nails and they will look after you.

# Men's Section

Some men may feel that they have no concerns about their body shape. Although women worry more about their shape than men, I feel it is important that men are aware of their body shapes, especially with regards to how they look and select clothes. The men that do have concerns about their body shape usually want to:

- change problem areas such as the chest, stomach, arms or legs.

- Increase muscle and its appearance.

- Loose fat and tone up.

There are a lot more men having cosmetic surgery performed to sculpture their bodies, including procedures such as liposuction, body wraps, weight training and specialised diets. Some men spend their money on designer and tailored outfits to enhance their body shape, (appreciated by women around the globe).

Men continue to have a mindset like Quentin,

*"...tall and proud, a full figure of a five-foot man, ...with a cuddly 14 stone chiselled physique."*

Work with what you have. Enjoy and appreciate the present.

During my research of body types, I came across three classifications that were new to me. They are often used to describe the physique of the male.

The classification is called **Somatotyping** and the body is defined using three factors:

1. **Ectomorphy** - Slenderness/thin. Represents the body types that are tall and slim. Individuals that can eat anything without gaining weight. Athletes, gymnasts, runners and dancers.

2. **Endomorphy** - Fatness/rounded/stout. Carries more fat around the body and usually find it hard to shift weight quickly, even if on strict calorie controlled diet. Swimmers, sports people.

3. **Mesomorphy** - Muscularity/athletic. Carry more muscle than fat on their frame. Strong, stocky, muscular build. Rugby players, sprinters.

Investing time and effort in enhancing your physique and the way you present yourself, can give you a great boost of confidence. Keep a sense of balance, if you are naturally slim. Fret not, not all women like muscles; personality, intellect, a smile, humour and common sense are also valuable assets to own.

 Here are a few tips to consider:

**Co ordination:** become aware of which colours compliment your skin and look good together. Avoid wearing too many bold patterned items, in the same outfit.

**Styles:** if you are buying an item in a style you have never worn before, try it on and be honest with yourself. Ask advice of a personal shopper or someone whose taste you admire.

**Cuts:** buy/wear clothes that emphasise your good points and disguise the weaker ones. For example, avoid wearing small, clingy lycra tops if you are overweight/have a large stomach. Instead buy a comfortable, fitting shirt, that has a lycra mix content.

For comfort, wear 100% cotton tee-shirts and when they become worn, misshapen or discoloured replace them.

Consider the type of neckline you wear. If you have a short, strong neck, avoid tight restrictive collars; experiment with V necked shirts and with lower front fastening garments. Men with long necks should avoid turtle necks. Common sense I hear you say, but you would be amazed at how many men, do not follow simple rules.

**Leg length:** try on trousers for fit, general look/the way they drape with shoes or boots. Pay particular attention to how they frame your bottom. Bend down and see if anything is exposed. Check how they hang from the waist, for puckering and gathering around the groin area;
sit down in them to see if they reveal too much of your socks. Many shops will do alterations for you. There is no excuse for poorly fitting trousers. Remember, different materials can hang differently, depending on the weight and cut of the fabric.

**Belts:** wear them appropriately; choose your correct size, and colour for the garment being worn.

**Shoes:** "shoes doth the man make." There is nothing worse than a well dressed man, wearing the wrong colour, or style of shoes, that are in bad condition. If your shoes have holes in them; have worn down heels; smell, or you have been wearing them for years; treat your self to a new pair. To a woman it might suggest, that you are not the total image you are attempting to portray.

**Grooming:** look good and smell good. Shower/wash at least twice a day, as body odours are not always apparent to you. The more activities you do, the more you are likely to sweat, so if in doubt bathe using a cleansing agent. Remember, if you eat strong flavoured foods, that can also come through in the sweat.

Get to know what smells goood on you. Everyone has
a particular body odour. Some women find male sweat
appealing, (due to the presence of Androstenol), but this
is only once the male has started sweating, not once the
sweat becomes stale. The majority of male sweat contains
Androstenone, which is not appealing and if not dealt with,
you could find yourself being far from popular. If you have
an excessive sweat problem, (called **Hyperhidrosis**), seek
medical advice. There has been much in the news about
possible links with deodorants causing health problems.
There are safer alternatives, slightly more expensive, but
worth the peace of mind.

When trying to find an aftershave or cologne, get general
advice from large department stores (aftershaves and
colognes counters). Listen to their advice on how to layer
your body correctly, starting with shower gels, aftershaves
and body sprays. Using products that smell similar, rather
than lots of different ones all together,
is a great benefit. I am blessed that my
husband embraced this long before
I met him and continues to do it so
well. Thanks honey.

Do not be fooled into believing, that
all women want the rough, rugged or
grungy looking guy.

They may well admire him, but that
does not mean they want to live
with him or take him home. Wearing
aftershaves can help to raise your
mood, giving you a sense of well-
being.

Shaving, regular hair washing and cuts, will complete the overall look. If you wear a beard or moustache, keep it neat, clean, combed and healthy. Get your barber to trim nose and ear hair at the same visit. Keeping toe and finger nails clean, is also a part of grooming. Having short clean nails is adequate. There is nothing wrong with getting a manicure or pedicure, if you feel like it. Taking personal pride in your appearance will pay dividends, believe me. Your partner/intended partner, will be eternally happy and grateful. You too, will be happy with you, which is the most important thing.

### Inner awareness

Quentin starts his day by affirming himself positively. He begins each day by telling himself good things:

***"Today" he told his reflection in the mirror, "is the start of something new."***

Making positive statements about ourselves, can change the way we think, act, speak, expect, or allow situations and people to affect us and treat us, on a daily basis.

It is amazing how many people struggle, when asked to say something good or positive about themselves, but if asked for their worst characteristics, the list would be so much longer. I want to challenge this behaviour and encourage you to change this mindset if you are guilty of it.

I always tell myself:

**"Something good is going to happen."**

Then if I know it is going to be a busy day, I smile and tell myself:

**"You can do this, watch out world here I come."**

When motivation is low and I do not feel my best, I put on something red, accessorise with a favourite piece of jewellery, finished off with the perfume that gets heads turning. I smile broadly at myself and say:

**"Looking good, best move out of my way because I am wearing red, and I am feeling dangerous."**

Red is my favourite colour, I wear it well, it makes me feel very passionate, purposeful and at times troublesome. Get to know what compliments you.

On the following page you will find a copy of an affirmation called "An Affirmation from God to You," (taken from a short article called "Butterfly come forth." © Janice Quashie 2004).

## An Affirmation from God to You.

God has esteemed **YOU** higher, than the value of
any precious gem on earth.

If others do not recognise your true worth,
your ministry, or whatever it is you want to achieve
for God, then do not bully them
into accepting your viewpoint.
Your gift will make room for you.

Actions will speak louder than words.
And with God's involvement you do not have to
bang your own drum.
Your humbleness will be exalted,
in God's way and His time.

There will come a time when with out pride,
vanity and self gratification you will exhibit the gift,
talent, skill that God has blessed you with.

When you establish a personal relationship
with God and you allow him to mature you,
your gift(s) will glorify God.

Until you give up everything,
in your pursuit to please God,
nothing will satisfy you.

© Janice Quashie 2004

Take some time and write an affirmation/positive statement about yourself. Make it something you will be proud of. Talk about your achievements and your best qualities; write them out, make them attractive, laminate and frame them. It may take some time to complete it fully, but keep writing and adding to it, until you are happy. Length is irrelevant. It is simply to raise your spirits, when you feel that you need a reminder of who you are. You might have more than one, so keep a wallet sized version for the car and larger copies for your work and home.

## Think about it

- Do you know who you are, or do you need people to validate (make you feel important/ value) you?

- Do you seek the approval of others?

- Do you let other peoples opinions of you change the way you act or feel about yourself?

- What can you do to change this?

- How could you manage this positively?

## MY AFFIRMATIONS

Date................................................................. .

.......................................................................
.......................................................................
.......................................................................
.......................................................................
.......................................................................
.......................................................................
.......................................................................
.......................................................................
.......................................................................
.......................................................................
.......................................................................
.......................................................................
.......................................................................
.......................................................................
.......................................................................

## Summary

1. Be aware of how colour, grooming, body image and posture affects your outlook.

2. Work on being positive about the way you talk and represent yourself.

3. Do your homework. Use the internet, magazines and books not to copy styles and fashions, but to learn tricks of the trade, concerning grooming, styling and presentation.

4. Be yourself, it is hard to constantly portray something you are not.

## Develop Better Relationships, Focusing on How I Relate to Others

Quentin is not fazed when people snub him, he simply says:

***"Their loss, they are running away from a good thing."***

His mind set does not allow him, to think that he has a problem. He does not wait for someone to dictate his sense of worth, he knows what they are missing. In life we often need to have waterproof, duck like skin; skin that allows negative and abusive words to flow over them; refusing to accept harsh words as truths. We are not talking about becoming so hard that nothing affects us, not thick or rhino skinned; but porous and flexible.

There are many adults carrying mental scars from negative statements said to them by school teachers, parents, friends, work colleagues, employers or enemies. Words and actions that have wounded them and left them bitter, frustrated, isolated adults. I have learnt not to give people, that power over my life. I am not saying that negative words do not hurt, because they can do. I am saying that I either totally disregard the statement, or I consider any elements that may be true and throw out the rest; always being aware of what I allow to affect me. I can only do this, because I am very aware of who I am, where I want to go and that I am far from being perfect, prone to making mistakes, but that I love me, with all my good and bad elements. I am a work in progress.

Inner health and awareness can be aided by remaining in a state of happiness and contentment. Positive mental attitude can help to keep us in good health. The immune system can be maintained healthily by reducing stressors, relaxing, sleeping well, eating a balanced diet, exercise and fitness. Looking back at my health, I know this is true. I maintain that sickness is not for me. I listen to my body when it gives out signals. If I am tired, regardless of the time of day, I will sleep or power nap. I can not deprive myself of sleep. Even when our first child was born, when she slept, so did I. Sleeping helps the cells repair and regenerate themselves. During this time the mind sorts, deletes and stores your thoughts and memories. Repeated lack of sleep can result in bad mood swings, irritability, changes in bowel habits and hormones; dry skin, eyes and hair...need I go on? Get to know your body and how it works. We do not function all the same way, there are individual differences. This is very important when considering taking medications.

When you have a good belly laugh, the whole immune system is given a work out. That simply means that the body releases hormones called endorphins, (they give you that feel good factor). Laughing causes you to relax, sends blood pumping quickly around the body and causes you to take deep breaths. Laugh on a daily basis: it can improve your resistance to colds, keep you looking younger, aid sleep, act as a natural pain relief and even help you to cope in stressful situations. I know from personal experience that looking at stressful situations light heartedly and even laughing at myself, has allowed me to regain my focus and handle stressful situations more positively. I believe it is the reason I do not look my age. I try to maintain a bright outlook as much as possible, but even I have down days. Dark winter days change my mood, but I either play inspiring music, dance, sing, go for a scenic walk, or do something creative to lift my spirit. If all else fails, I head for a good dose of sunshine.

If you believe in prayer, then praying can help you enter your day in a calm, focused, positive state of mind. We have become so interested in what we can get next, that we forget to give thanks for the here and now.

Try this beautiful exercise I experienced, in a prayer room. Find a stop watch, clock or watch with a second hand. Do this exercise in a quiet, place where you will not be disturbed. Make yourself comfortable and watch the seconds go by, for one whole minute. During that time think, focus on watching time go by and try not to be distracted by thoughts. For another minute, focus on God and pray a prayer, thanking him for right now. Forget about past events and hurts; do not think about what might happen or what you want to happen; just thank him for the moment you are in.

It is amazing how difficult it can be, to concentrate on the here and now, without bringing up our past, or our future, other people, or events. The more you do this exercise, the better your prayers of thankfulness will become. There is no hidden agenda, just heart felt gratitude and praise, for the miracle of being alive and recognition of the awesomeness of God.

Alternatively, if you find prayer difficult, try meditating with music, or a piece of text that you find serene and beautiful.

There will always be busy, anxious people on your way to work, or school, at the shops, but do not let their state of mind, cause you to loose your calmness and serenity, as that will then set the tone for the day.

Work relationships often cause people a lot of concern. The more people you work with, the harder it seems to be.

Do you try to fit in, by being one character with this group of friends/colleagues, whilst wearing another mask with others? That can be tiring and confusing. You have to learn which persona goes where and you eventually forget who you really want to be, in your quest to fit in. When you have good self-esteem and you know who you are, then you can challenge or correct anyone, who may try to discredit, belittle, or insult you. You do not have to keep changing to suit people or their opinions. (This includes parents, partners and family members, no matter how hard it maybe).

Keep it simple. Do not try to be all things to all people. Do not try to change yourself to be accepted, it is a pointless exercise. You have to be true to who you are and if you are consistent, people will grow to like, understand and appreciate you, or just accept that you are different. There will always be people who do not like you, that is their prerogative, just maintain a level of being civil and a professional working relationship. Not everyone at work needs to be in your personal space. Having good self-esteem makes you seem confident, even when you are not. You are able to listen to the views of others, but remain true to you and your values. Make sure you give your opinion, as silence can often be read as consent and if you continually do this, people stop asking you and assume they can answer for you. You will hear "Oh don't worry she/he will do it. No need to ask, they always do." Do not let yourself be taken for granted, you never know who is watching. You could be destroying any future chances of promotion. People often want me to tone down my flamboyant, naughty character, but I just have to be me, nothing else feels right. If a prospective partner is watching, they will love not only your physical attributes, but your sense of character and personality.

Do not be like Quentin who has no apparent interest in his work acquaintances, but loves tea and biscuits. Make the most of your work environment, you spend enough time there.

What ever Quentin does, he does it with a spirit of excellence; he is keen and eager.
When was the last time you were excited about something work or course related? Does your work reflect your inner flare?

Do you go the extra mile in work, college, school, or do you just do the expected, the bare minimum?
What will set you apart from others?

Impress yourself, I always do, it gives me personal satisfaction. I try not to worry about people who tease, or call me swotty, it usually means there is either jealousy on their part, or that they are feeling that I am highlighting their inadequacies. Either way, that is their hang up not mine. I take personal pride in everything I do, it reflects who I am and who I represent. I do things to the best of my ability; because of my creative side, it can often be seen as a little dramatic. Impact is a great thing at times. In a work environment doing a basic job as specified, is a good standard of practice, but if given creative licence, put your personal stamp on it and enjoy that feeling of satisfaction that comes with completion.

What kind of impression do you make?
Do you blend into the background?
In your work/life environment do people know you exist?
Do people know your name? Do they use it?
How do they refer to you?

Ask people to use your name. As a student nurse I would often remind some hospital consultants, doctors and even patients that my name was not "Nursie," or "You there," or "Staff," or "Could you just get me…" I repeated my name and on some occasions refused to acknowledge them, until I heard a proper address. Treat others as you want to be treated, in an assertive, non-aggressive manner. This will ensure people take you seriously.

Most of us were given names at birth, but so many of us allow people to chop up, shorten, mispronounce, or rename us. If you are happy with that, then this does not apply to you. Having an unusual name can be complicated for some people, but do not make excuses for people. If you say it enough times, they will get it. It is usually just laziness on their part. Be proud of your name, what ever culture or country you come from. Names have meanings. Look yours up and see if the meaning is a part of your character. Janice and Ian, (that's my husband's name), have the same meaning – "God is gracious/God's grace," Hebrew in origin. If the meaning of your name is not fitting, or you have a name that is not in a book, create your own meaning.

Check your posture; the way you stand and walk speak volumes. People watch your body language and stature. What is your body language saying?

Do you walk looking down? If yes, then you need to stand upright. Do not lean or hunch yourself forward. Make a conscious effort to be aware of where your shoulders are. Push your chest slightly forward. Keep your head up, see the obstacles before they hit you. Everything has rhythm and pace, so walk with purpose, think of your posture, keeping an even pace and stride. Think of how special and unique you are, walk with an air of confidence. People with high self-esteem often appear to walk tall and being of shorter statue, walking tall can add height to you. Let your body language suggest that you are positive, even if you are not feeling particularly confident. Those watching will see you differently, compared to an image of head down, shoulders hunched and no eye contact.

This is a good technique to use when entering an unknown environment, meeting new people, or in a interview situation.

It always works well when speaking to a room of people. If you get nervous, instead of looking at all the faces, find a focal point on the other side of the room, just above their heads, so it looks like you are looking directly at them. Let your body language speak for you, let it match what you will verbally say, long before you open your mouth.

If you get tongue tied and anxious around strangers, take a deep calming breath and listen carefully before you speak. Try smiling slightly before you answer, to give yourself time to formulate your thoughts in your mind. Remember the other person may be nervous too.

Your handshake can also betray you. You want to give a firm handshake, so that the other person knows that contact has been made. Avoid bone crushing, it is not impressive, just painful. Limp wrist/barely touching syndrome can appear snobbish or offensive.

## Pause for Thought

Be careful if you:

- Make sweeping statements,

- Make judgements based on first meetings,

- Make assumptions, based on your gut feelings

- Stereotype people and situations with out getting more information.

You could miss out on developing solid friendships. Or broaden your character by learning about cultures, beliefs, and interests different to your own. Knowledge is power. Prejudice and discrimination will only be removed when, we get rid of our quick to judge nature. I am sure someone has misjudged you at least once, give someone a second chance. They may surprise you, or just confirm what you think you first felt. Remember they could just be having a bad day.

## An Emotional Check-Up

> **Emotion** - disturbance of mind, mental sensation or state, instinctive feeling as opposed to reason
>
> **Emotional** - of or related to the emotions, expressing emotion, liable to excessive emotion.
>
> Concise Oxford Dictionary

In everything we need to keep a sense of balance. I feel the importance of maintaining emotional well-being has been overlooked, which is why we see so many people suffering from mental ill health, depression, stress, relationship break downs and anxiety disorders. Which was why I became a freelance Emotional Health Consultant, to help people to cope with their emotional issues.

I can honestly say that I have lived through a series of strange and often frightening emotions, since I decided to write this book. On reflection, my whole life has been tied up with other peoples feelings and emotions. People seem to naturally gravitate to me. Total strangers come up to me and begin to ask my advice on deeply personal issues, or share their life story. It has been said that I have a sense of wisdom and insight (simply what used to be called common sense). I believe it is a gift from God that I use, to encourage, empower and enrich the lives of those, who I am blessed to assist and work with.

There are so many people today who act in anger, in competitive mode, or by simply letting their emotions run away with them. In stressful situations, Quentin gives himself a chance to calm down, think and then act rationally, not impulsively. Try it the next time you are angry or frustrated.

Angry or emotional outbursts can cause a lot of pain, misunderstanding and grief. Think. Is it worth risking a friendship just to prove a point?

Women are often seen as the more emotional of the species. Biologically we do have more hormones roaming about the body, than the male. That I believe is something to celebrate. Having the ability to empathise, care, love whole heartedly, express openly how you feel, are fantastic female attributes that need to be respected by women firstly and recognised by men, not belittled, made excuses for or ridiculed.
I am not saying that men don't have these same qualities - some do, but they are presented differently. Even the media has been covering stories about men, who have been so stressed that they have had to cry in public. Why is that so unbelievable? Men are affected by emotion. For too long, men have been brought up to suppress showing outward emotion. Maybe more relationships would be blooming and healthy, if a few more male tears were shed, a little vulnerability was shown, or verbal expression of true feelings were expressed. Well let us leave that there, shall we?

However, there are many women with stunted emotional development, who have been affected by:

- breakdown in relationships.
- sexual attack.
- poor/absent male role models.
- being deceived, rejected.
- not being chosen.
- trying to find love with numerous sexual partners.
- violence in relationships.
- verbal abuse.

- living lives where they refuse to recognise that they are passionate sensuous beings, capable of giving and receiving love and passion.

Having the ability to be emotional, is a strength, not a weakness. Keeping a sense of balance, helps us to express how we feel with out seeming hysterical, over the top, or fanatical. I am proud to be emotional and passionate. It shows I am alive and a woman of strength and character. I cry, laugh, show anger, disappointment, sadness, joy... Can you?

There are just as many men who are bound by emotions, some are not aware, others in denial and the remainder are unsure of what to do. They too have been:

- abused.
- attacked.
- hurt in relationships.
- misunderstood.
- told that expressing emotion is weakness.

They are often portrayed as angry, aggressive, unemotional and unsympathetic. Emotions are a release mechanism for the body. How you express that is personal to you. There are some very balanced men, who know how to express themselves well. They have learnt to keep track on how their emotional state affects them and others. They are good communicators and listeners and make the best friends, partners and husbands.

I wrote a poem called Who Am I? , which expresses where you may eventually want to be , as you develop emotional balance.

# WHO AM I ?

I am more than what you see,
I am more than what you hear about me.
More than what you think you know of me.

I am not my past. Events in my life have
moulded, wounded and affected me.

I am not my visual image, as that changes like
the weather.

I am not even the various personas I take on
to get me through the day.

The real me is the part you don't see,
The spiritual part, my mind, soul and heart.

Spend time with me, invest in me;
Share, laugh, and rest with me.
Then in time you won't need to ask,
Who am I, for you will know;
I am a creative work in progress, designed
by God just the way He intended.

© Janice Quashie 2005

If you are the kind of person who has anger issues; who continually flies off the handle; is affected daily by road rage; or becomes impatient with people; then you may want to consider getting professional help with the management of your anger. There are books and courses available on this topic.

Getting angry is not a problem, (healthy expression of annoyance reduces the incidence of psychological and physical symptoms), but the way in which you express your anger can be. There are people who get so cross, that they cause their blood pressure to rise, get headaches and some get visual disturbances and see a dark area or red mist, before they verbally, or physically attack others. Be honest with yourself and open enough to hear when someone is brave enough, to point out that you are aggressive, hot tempered or angry. It could be rectified by simply lowering the volume or speed at which you speak; developing a warmer tone; or smiling (not grimacing), more.
Try to work out if there are triggers that cause you to become angry. Are there issues from your past, that you have not dealt with? Are there people that you need to forgive and let go? Do you need a holiday, regular relaxation sessions, or a change of direction in life or work? Do you need to delegate work, or seek training to help you cope with the demands of work? Take your time and work through your issues, one by one. Many will be linked, so it might be quicker to resolve the issues than you think.

## Anger Management Exercise

- Be honest about what triggers your anger/aggression - try to work out alternative ways of expressing anger.

- Forgive yourself and others. Remaining angry and bitter leaves you defeated and powerless. It takes away your energy.

- Learn to channel your aggression/anger into sporting activities. Kick boxing, aerobics, karate, judo, self defence and weight lifting. Other activities could include bread making and gardening - especially pulling up weeds, rubbish clearance and digging. When angered walk away from the situation and use the anger to do tasks that you normally have difficulty doing, e.g. paper sorting, clearing cupboards, cleaning and dusting.

One thing that amazes me about love and emotion is its amazing power to change people and the way they react. Love and emotion have the ability to disarm you and captivate you, quickly, silently and painlessly. They do not care about your age, race, colour, status or education. They strike when you least expect or need them.
How many like Quentin, have been taken by surprise by love, or found themselves doing or saying things to some one they have liked and have then wondered;
"Why did I do that?" or "why am I feeling this way?"

Admit it, we have all had daydreams about someone we have liked and found ourselves wondering, what they like and what they do when you are apart. It is all part of expressing healthy emotions. Do not try to deny or suppress them. No matter what age, or particular phase your life is in; whether you are looking for love or not; when it decides it is time, then you are hooked. Just enjoy every emotion, feeling and sensation that being in love evokes. Keep a mental picture of how you feel and keep that glow alive, keep passion alive on a daily basis.

When you initially communicate with people, you may find your first impressions of them were totally wrong. Often when we are attracted to someone, we deny positive feelings, because we fear being rejected, ridiculed or embarrassed, if they do not feel the same way. The best relationships begin as friendships. Get to know people, by spending time with them. If you feel attracted to someone, never just take things at face value. Get to know what is under the skin, meaning, find out what makes them tick, what moves them, their passions, dreams, goals, achievements, views on life, politics, family, marriage, their history. Far too many people rush into relationships and then get hurt, disillusioned and frustrated when their beloved reveals their true colours. Take the time to find out whether or not to reveal your true feelings. There are thousands of people with bad relationship experiences out there. Remember, marriage/ relationships are full of surprises. Getting to know and tolerate a partner's true personality and coping with it positively on a daily basis, is all part of the journey called marriage, or cohabiting.

Friendships can also be difficult relationships for some adults, especially if they feel they emotionally attach themselves to others and then become needy, or a burden. A good friendship needs balance, respect of each others personal space and time. Very few people want to spend every waking minute, in one person's company - it only causes feelings of resentment, being closed in and reduces interesting communication. Interaction with others, living life and being active, adds to the fabric of our relationships.

If you believe that you attach yourself to others consider:

- Asking your friends to tell you, if you outstay your welcome. Limit the time you stay and leave at a decent time.

- Increasing your network of friends.

- Looking at why you feel the need to rely heavily on particular people.

- Finding new hobbies and activities, (e.g. sports, holidays, outings and groups), that involve new people. Become active in other areas of your life.

Although it may be hard to be this honest with yourself, it may help you to keep those valuable friendships. Truth can be difficult for anyone to take, but if spoken in love, then receive it that way.

There are times when it is good to act on impulse, when you need to acknowledge and react to, that strange gut feeling or instinct. One could say that Quentin missed out on a good opportunity. Why did he not just ask for her telephone number? Given those circumstances, most people would have wanted to ask but would have been stopped by fear of rejection, stress and anxiety, shyness and childish behaviour.

Like a true fighter, Quentin does not waste time worrying about what could have been. He quickly brushes himself off and moves on to new things. I believe that there is a time for everything and often, what seems like a missed opportunity, may in your future come around again to be a wonderful reality. Who knows how or where Quentin's, and Clarissa's paths may cross again, only time will tell!!!

## Pause for Thought

**Do you hold on to disappointments?**

**Do you allow failure to disable you?**

**Are criticisms from the past still haunting and hurting you?**

**Have you continued to beat yourself with the same critical stick that others used to use on you?**

**If you answered yes to any of these questions, then you need to give yourself the license to forgive others and move on. Forgiving and allowing yourself the opportunity and freedom to enjoy life.**

---

## Discover purpose/goals for your life; activating and fulfilling them

**Purpose** - the reason for which something is done, or for which something exists.

Concise Oxford Dictionary

---

When life has purpose, it has meaning. There has to be a point to doing things, otherwise things seem pointless and worthless. Do you have a purpose or goal for your life?

For many setting goals and planning are time consuming endless tasks. This is your future you are planning for. Make the time, make it exciting, you have to live it. The alternative is to let life pass you by and moan about how boring and repetitive things are.

### Focused

Quentin had dreams. They were active dreams; he was planning how to make them reality, how to find himself a partner. Do you have active dreams?

Far too many people drift through life too busy working, to give themselves something to look forward to. It is always "I will plan something next week, next month, next year." Before you know it, you stop dreaming and continue through life until you start to say, "That's life, that's just the way it is, nothing I can do about it now." Making dreams become reality requires planning, action, and evaluation.

What should you plan for?

Finance - major investments
Education
Leisure - holidays
Career
Retirement
Weddings
Funerals
Children
Redundancy
Sickness
The unexpected

The list is endless, so choose one thing, plan it out, begin the process of making changes and before you know you will be multi planning.

Quentin is able to re-think his problems, re-group and come back to face the problem again from a different angle. Despite what he is faced with, he never gives up. He is a tryer, with determination and the spirit to succeed.
What fazes you? What stops you from achieving what you want to in life?

Stress comes to attack Quentin through various physical symptoms: nausea, faintness, loss of speech, loss of bodily control, sweating and difficulty breathing. When fear, stress or anxiety grip you, how do you react? Do you control the stress or does it control you?

Quentin has enough self-awareness to know that regardless of the stress, he must complete the task before him. When anxiety strikes, come away from the stressful environment: take a walk; have a warm drink; do deep breathing; listen to relaxing music; before attempting to go back to it.

Like many people, Quentin is resistant to change. He does a lot of things in his working day routinely and is put out if things change. Change is good, it keeps us on our toes and makes sure our brains are given a daily work. It allows us to use common sense principles and problem solving skills, which enable us to plan our personal and professional developments. Never become so rigid and inflexible, that if change occurs, you become less able to function. Be adaptable, practical, forward thinking. If there are gaps in your knowledge or you notice a particular area of weakness, ask your line manager for training. Pick courses you want to go on, before you present your case to the management. Do your own personal research.

Even when faced with obstacles Quentin is not stopped. He sets his mind on the task ahead and he goes out of his way to obtain his prize. He is not put off by unfamiliar faces; he keeps his goal in view and then uses his skills to manoeuvre him into position.

When faced with an obstacle Quentin does not instinctively react. He takes himself out of the situation, gives himself time to think and compose himself. He re-assesses, evaluates and formulates a new plan and then implements it. Try it, it works.

Quentin can still appreciate the small details. He finds joy
in simple pleasures, like whistling and custard creams.
When we become so wrapped up in our own problems
and the need to meet deadlines and targets, then little
things can become a chore. To appreciate the here and
now, we need to stop looking at the whole situation,
and begin to see the picture in smaller more manageable
chunks. This makes tasks seem easier to achieve; gives
you time to value and enjoy what you are doing; and may
give you the opportunity to delegate, or include others in
the process.

Using or creating documents that are written or printed,
will allow others to learn and use the process for
themselves. Documents can be referred to and reviewed
on set dates. This will help you chart progress made,
unachieved goals and unexpected outcomes.

## Quentin's Overview

For those of you wondering about Quentin's love of
his chair, all I can say is we all need a passion in life.
For some it is pets, art, food, children, work, hobbies;
for Quentin it is his chair. Like an antique dealer he
appreciates the craftsmanship of the noble chair he sits
in. He is aware of how much attention antiques need to
preserve them.

Like many people, he wants love, support and stability;
some-one to be there when he needs them; and someone to share and lavish tenderness on. The world can be
a cruel and lonely place for people like Quentin, who
do not fit the rich, good looking, jet setting category of
people. Despite this fact, Quentin had decided that until

he could find someone to give his love to, he would value other things.

People find their stability in a number of places: alcohol, drugs, gambling, sex, themselves. My faith in God is my stabiliser; God keeps my mind, body and spirit focused on a daily basis, so I can trust him for everything. What do you depend on? What is your stabilising factor? Remember, no-one has to share or believe in you, or your dreams, but you. Live the dream and have the courage to make it a reality, (as many people told me, when I wrote "A True Love Story"), and you are holding that dream in your hands.

# A True Love Story

## Section 3

# My True Love Story

**True** - in accordance with fact or reality, not false or erroneous.

**Love** - warm affection, attachment, liking, or fondness, affectionate devotion.

True love. Is it a truth, reality or myth? Many have spent their lives, time and money in search of true love, wanting to prove or disprove its existence.

Like many of you, I too wanted to find true love. For me, true love represented a time, place and a person. I would know when I had found true love, because the timing would be perfect and things would be going well in all areas of my life. The setting would be idyllic, tranquil, beautiful and just right. True love would be a person who would love me no matter what, despite my past and my faults; who would embrace and enhance the very essence, spirit, fabric, every fibre that made me, me. Ah true love! a song, poem, story, fragrance, drink, colour or sensation. True love would be life in total completeness, happiness and constant joy. True love would engulf me, caress me, protect, support and cheer me; be dedicated and faithful to me. That was how I saw true love, with youthful innocent eyes.

Years and life experiences have moulded my views and changed the somewhat romantic notions of true love into...

Let us take a look back over my 40 years and see how many times true love made an appearance.

My mother gave me the first examples, of what true love involved. My mother, a living angel with a naughty streak.

A smile and disposition that could warm the coldest heart and room, and a dangerous side, that if provoked would send you running for cover. I learnt from my mother, that true love always sees the best in everything and everyone. My mother fought to preserve her marriage and family life for the sake of her children. She endured physical and mental abuse, yet still maintained her faith in God and in the sanctity of marriage. Where was true love in all of this you ask?

True love represented dedicating your life to those you love and to those who refuse to love you back. True love represented believing, despite what you saw, heard or felt. True love for my mother was hard work, a lonely place, laying aside personal dreams and goals to encourage, support and love others selflessly. Today my mother pursues life wholeheartedly. She embraced her dream to write and publish her first book. She teaches, encourages and travels. God has, and remains her True Love, because he has been there for her when no one else could be.

My first personal introduction to true love, came in the form of Tonka toys. I loved them so! My toy truck collection was invaluable. They were strong, indestructible, reliable and according to the advert, could withstand an elephants weight. The trucks however, were no match for my two brothers, who made it their personal goal in life to destroy them. There ended my first love affair.

True love made a brief appearance in my infant school. He came in the form of a little Caucasian boy. True love is unaware of colour, race or creed, especially in the early years of innocence. We went everywhere together: the sand pit, book corner, milk table and the play ground. We held hands whilst the teacher read in the story corner. Alas, true love came to an end when his family emigrated to a warmer climate. Looking back now, even at that young age, I decided never to love anyone again, because their leaving would take a piece of me way, just like the little boy had. Strangely enough, I never had boyfriends or entertained affection from them during my formative years. I protected my heart and my feelings, by locking them behind an electrified fence of " I don't need nobody, I don't want a man, I'm never going to get married," barbed wire.

I looked for true love in my father's eyes and heart. Stress, anxiety, depression, mental health problems and other peoples opinions, robbed him of his joy for life and left him unable to help or love me. True love showed me that there are times when for the sake of your sanity, you have to let the people you love, go their own way. Especially when the relationship causes pain and distress. I tried in vain for years to break through the walls my father had put around himself. I wanted him to be like other fathers, to clap for me at the school play, to play ball with me and chase off young men that came to ask me out. Despite being pushed out of his life by the mental health, true love persuaded me to ask my father to give me away. On my wedding day, the day that should have been the happiest of my life, moments before walking down the aisle, my father ushered his parting blessing. Words that at the time, hit me to my very soul, yet freed me to be a person in my own right, no longer looking for his approval, acknowledgement or love.

When the Vicar said, "Who gives this woman, to be married to this man?" and my father replied "I do" and gave my hand to my husband, true love freed me and my heart. I left at the altar all my hurts and regrets and walked away with my true love.

Sometimes you have to go back to go forward, so let us go back briefly to my single days. As a teenager, I had vowed that:

1) No man was going to dump me.
2) That I would not bow to the peer pressures of smoking, drinking, gambling, making out behind the bike sheds, or the back seat of a car.
3) No man was going to give me a love bite.
4) I would never marry.

I became a studious teenager, with no nonsense ideals. My mother always said that "I didn't suffer fools gladly," which simply meant that I had no time for time wasters, idiots, or childish behaviour. I read and learnt endless information and studied people who had words of wisdom, lived life's overcoming struggles and yet persevered.

We went to Sunday School and Churches from an early age and some how I knew that God was there for me, especially during the nights when my father had his episodes and I prayed in fear, asking God to keep my family safe until morning.

God became my true love, who loved me unconditionally despite my mistakes. True love changed my life and thinking during a meeting, when a preacher preached a simple message that helped me resist temptation and retain my virginity. It was a message without shouting or sweating. He spoke gently and openly about things that keep you spiritually bound and tied. I paid little attention to the first part of his sermon, but he grabbed my attention when he said "sex is best in a loving marital relationship." He explained that although the world was advocating free love and casual sex, when you have sexual intercourse with someone that you are not married to, you develop soul ties or spiritual connections; not only with them, but with the other people they had slept with. He also went onto explain the risks of pregnancy and developing sexually transmitted infections. He explained that lovemaking should occur within the bounds of marriage and was created by God, to be enjoyed with the person to whom you had decided to become one with. Sexual intimacy, was giving yourself freely and lovingly to each other. The end result being a new life stemming from both of you. From that point onwards, I had no desire to join myself with anyone.

This information helped me to refrain from sexual activity and **I pledged to myself,** that I would wait until I found true love within marriage. I was never going to be a notch on someone's bedpost, nor taken advantage of by a sweet talking guy, who only wanted what he could not have: the challenge of a Christian virgin. Ladies, never fall for a guy who tells you that if you love him, you would sleep with him. Young men, don't do it just because everyone else says they are. Respect yourself enough to say no, especially to anyone who suggests that alcohol or drugs will relax you during sex. If it feels wrong, follow your gut instinct. True love allows you to be yourself, enjoying passion and sexual relationships without guilt or pain.

True love takes many forms through out your life. Embrace it when it comes. Allow yourself the freedom to experience true love fully and unashamedly.

# A True Love Story

# Section 4

I have included this section in the book, just for you. I hope that by the time you have read the True Love Story and worked your way through the workbook sections, that you will feel inspired to create your own masterpiece. "Your True Love Story," has two purposes:

1. For those who had difficulty accepting the original ending of "A True Love Story," feel free to take the opportunity to write an ending that makes you happy. Feel free to share them with me at **janicequashie@ msn.com** and I will show them on my website: **www.atruelovestory.org**

Or

2. Write your own story. Who knows where it may take you or what you might reveal about yourself? There maybe a budding writer in you.

Many people drift through life without taking notice of the events that occur. Experience has taught me, that these events provide the building blocks of your emotional development.

We believe sometimes that we can remember most of the events that go on in our lives. The mind is an incredible tool. It has the ability to store, catalogue and erase memories, or events. The older we get and the more crowded our minds become, the less space there is for memory storage. We can loose memories that could be important because there is no space for them. This is where these pages come in. Seeing your thoughts, ideas, happenings, dreams, goals, or plans, written down; with pictures, illustrations, photographic images, swatches of material, flowers, etc., can be inspirational, educational, revealing, therapeutic and life changing. Not only do you have a permanent record of what happened for you to refer to, you can also create a family heirloom or a piece of history, telling and sharing your story, to generations to come. You may create a structure for a book, short story, website, club or business idea. The creative possibilities are endless.

Remember, you are important and if you do not appreciate yourself, respect yourself or love yourself, then how can you expect that from others?
This is not an easy process and it may mean facing, or revealing fears that you have kept hidden. Expose those fears, deal with them, get help sorting them out. You will eventually feel liberated, happier and more focused. Live life without regrets and hang ups. Do things that confirm that you are alive. Make your life worth living.

Use the following pages as suggestions or templates. Feel free to reproduce them, adapt or add to them. Create documents on your computer, in a notebook , journal or folder.

Now its your turn…

**Name**            **Date**                    **Daily Thoughts**

**My Alternative Ending to "A True Love Story"**

'The evaluation form filling drew near, signifying the end
of the session. The strange sensation returned to Quentin's
chest and he wondered if he dared ask for Clarissa's
contact details.

As he was pondering Clarissa said:
"Oh well, it was good to meet you Quentin. Thank you for
making this a memorable customer care session. Maybe
we will meet up at the next annual general meeting."

Before Quentin could summon up enough spittle to
lubricate his tongue, she floated past him and was gone.

He breathed a deep sigh and looked slightly sad and
reflective.'

........................................................................................

........................................................................................

........................................................................................

........................................................................................

........................................................................................

........................................................................................

........................................................................................

........................................................................................

........................................................................................

..............................................................................

..............................................................................

..............................................................................

..............................................................................

..............................................................................

..............................................................................

..............................................................................

..............................................................................

..............................................................................

..............................................................................

..............................................................................

..............................................................................

..............................................................................

..............................................................................

..............................................................................

..............................................................................

# My Story     **Date**

........................................................................................
........................................................................................
........................................................................................
........................................................................................
........................................................................................
........................................................................................
........................................................................................
........................................................................................
........................................................................................
........................................................................................
........................................................................................
........................................................................................
........................................................................................
........................................................................................
........................................................................................
........................................................................................
........................................................................................
........................................................................................
........................................................................................
........................................................................................
........................................................................................
........................................................................................
........................................................................................
........................................................................................
........................................................................................

**Personal Development Portfolio**

This section is an on going project and the information will change throughout your life, according to the experiences and encounters you go through. I suggest that once you have written each section, that you sign and date them. Then, put a review date to re-read and update them. I find this a particularly interesting exercise, as you get to see how your ideals change with age and maturity. It reminds you of where you have been and where you thought life was taking you to. Feel free to photocopy the form on the following pages, or to customise them.

There are so many books/resources on life coaching and self development. Why not take a trip to the library, book shop, or the internet and find further helpful tips, forms and suggestions?

Keep things short, sweet and simple.

Name …………………............... Date ………………………

| What are your strengths? | Review date |
|---|---|
| Physical Goals | |
| Mental Goals | |
| Spiritual Goals | |
| Emotional Goals | |

| What are my dreams? | |
|---|---|
| Creative Ideas | |
| Relaxation Activities | |
| Work Related Planner | |
| Study Days | |
| Financial Planning | |

| Financial Planning cont'd | |
| --- | --- |
| Personal Goals | |
| Relationships | |

## Who Do You Think You Are?

If raising your self-esteem is an issue for you, try this exercise.

Take 3 sheets of large paper. Write one of the titles listed below at the top of each page:

1) Who Am I?

2) How do people see me?

3) My dreams and goals?

Write or draw things that represent each of these areas.

Look carefully at your 3 sheets.

Compare sheets 1and 2.

Are they similar? Do you recognise yourself?

Are there changes you want to make?

How will you accomplish the changes?

Do you know the real you?

How do you want people to see you?

Look at sheet 3 and ask yourself:

What is preventing me from making my dreams/goals a reality?

# Contact Details

Thank you for taking the time to buy and read this book.
I hope that it has given you as much joy and tears reading
it, as it did to create it. If "A True Love Story" has awoken,
blessed or annoyed you, then its all good. That means that
you are still alive and able to feel emotion.

For those who feel creative - please send me an email of
your thoughts, reflections and feelings and I will post the
best ones on my website. Please state whether permission is
given to include the information on the website.

---

## Your Thoughts...

How did you react to the story and why?
Were you angry? Why?
Did you find it humorous? Why?
Did you recognise characteristics that reflect your
personality? Why?
Read the story again slowly picking out things that are
important to you.
Create a plan of action.

---

If you would like to arrange one to one sessions, group
discussions or speaking invitations, then email your contact
details/requirements and a suitable package will be provided
for you, at a great price.

Email: **janicequashie@ msn.com**
Website: **www.atruelovestory.org**

## About the Author

Janice Quashie is a qualified Nurse and Non practicing Midwife. She began following her dream to be a full time writer in 2004. She divides her time between her home, family and church, and her work as a freelance Emotional Health Consultant, for her project Strongtower Worldwide Link. Her role involves working with individuals who are stressed, depressed, or suffering with mental health problems, providing much needed support, practical advice and encouragement. She also has a passion for relationship issues and supports initiatives that provide sexual health advice and education for young people and their parents.

Working with communities in the UK and Ghana, has given Janice a wonderful insight into creative ways to help hurting people, recover hope, joy and peace of mind.

Her faith and her trust in God keeps her humble, human and humorous.

ISBN 141209589-1